CW00400689

1

RORY

I t was only a few months after the death of my parents, and I was lonelier than I ever remembered being. Wolves were social creatures by nature, and the same was true for wolf shifters. We were supposed to create close bonds with our families and packs, but I had always felt a barrier between my packmates and me. When I was old enough to understand everyone treated me differently, I assumed it was because my parents had broken the alpha's rules a few times, and nobody wanted to risk their reputation for trouble rubbing off on them.

Although they were no longer around to cause any trouble, the stain of being a Parker still remained. Wherever I went, I was reminded how unwanted I was in the place where I should have felt most welcome in the world. A simple trip to the grocery store wasn't even safe.

As I neared the entrance, a woman walking through the doors wrapped her fingers around her daughter's wrist to drag her to the opposite side of her body so she was between us.

"You almost made me drop my lollipop, Mama," the little girl complained.

"Sorry, sweetie." The woman's wolf flashed in her eyes as she glared at me. "But we need to hurry since they'll apparently let just anyone shop here."

She was acting as if my problems were somehow contagious. Not that she or anyone around here actually understood what I was going through when the alpha's son had them all convinced I was a horrible person.

Ignoring the irritated grumble of my wolf inside my head, I went into the store and grabbed a cart. After grabbing a few fruits and vegetables from the produce section, I rolled my cart to the meat counter. Nobody waited ahead of me, but the butcher ignored me for several minutes before heaving a deep sigh and asked, "Did you need something?"

"Yes, I'd like some venison." Lifting my chin, I stood tall as I met his gaze. "Three pounds of tenderloin."

OVER THE MOON

ROCHELLE PAIGE

Copyright © 2023 by Rochelle Paige

Cover designed by Elle Christensen

Edited by Editing4Indies

All rights reserved.

No part of this book may be reproduced in any form or by any electronic or mechanical means, including information storage and retrieval systems, without written permission from the author, except for the use of brief quotations in a book review.

❦ Created with Vellum

OVER THE MOON

Jared Oakes was surrounded by happily mated couples, but he wasn't sure he'd ever find his. As the beta to the head of the shifter council, he had traveled around the world and back again without discovering the woman who was meant to be his...until Rory Parker came to their pack for protection from the alpha's son who wanted to claim her as his own.

Rory didn't have a plan when she fled her pack in the middle of the night, but it turned out to be the best decision she'd ever made. Fate sent her running straight into the arms of her mate.

"Sorry," he murmured, not sounding the least bit apologetic. "All I have for you is some neck."

I glanced at the case and shook my head as I stared at the rows of cuts that were much more tender than the neck. "Really?"

"Like I said, I can give you three pounds of venison neck." He tilted his head toward the case. "The tenderloin is already spoken for by members of the pack."

"You mean *other* members, right?" I challenged, crossing my arms against my chest. "Since I'm also a part of the pack."

"Barely," he muttered.

As tempting as it was to point out the flaw in his logic, I knew that arguing further wouldn't do me a lick of good. So I just shrugged and said, "The neck meat will be fine."

He cut a piece of butcher paper off the roll, dropped a big chunk onto it, and sloppily taped it shut before slapping a price sticker on the side. Shoving the package at me, he grumbled, "Here."

The rest of my shopping trip was uneventful, right up until I reached the line for the cashier, and Sarah put the closed sign on her belt. There wasn't another register open, so I pushed it out of my way while I unloaded my cart. Then I stared at her until she started to ring me up with a huff.

"That'll be one hundred and ten dollars."

I glanced at the total on the display and shook my head. Handing her fifty dollars less, I muttered, "Nice try."

She shrugged, completely unbothered over being caught upcharging me by so much. "I was charging you the bitch tax."

"Jealousy isn't a good look on you," I chided as I stuffed my items into bags since Sarah couldn't be bothered to do it for me.

"As if," she gasped, narrowing her eyes. "I have nothing to be jealous of when it comes to you. Nobody can even stand to be around you."

I quirked a brow. "We both know there's one person who wishes he was much closer to me, and that's why you hate me so much. You would do just about anything to be Elijah's mate and couldn't care less if you were actually fated to be together or not."

My accusation was spot on, and she pressed her lips together in a flat line, finally choosing to back off. I was proud of standing up for myself as I walked out of the store, but the feeling only lasted until I spotted Elijah leaning against the driver's door of my car. He was the last person I wanted to see, especially when I was already irritated from how I was just treated.

Rounding the other side of my car, I popped my trunk and set my bags inside. Then I slammed the door shut and glared at my alpha's son. "Move."

"Is that any way to talk to your fated mate?" he asked, crossing one ankle over the other in a casual pose.

Swiveling my head, I made a big show of scanning the parking lot. There wasn't anyone else around, and I shrugged. "If the man I was fated to spend my life with was here, you can be sure that he'd love what I had to say to him. Unfortunately for me, I haven't met him yet."

Elijah pushed away from my car, his wolf flashing in his eyes. Beating his fist against his chest, he growled, "But you have. I'm right here, dammit."

"It doesn't matter how often you say we're supposed to be mates, your claim won't suddenly become true." I held my hand up to show him how steady it was. "If my wolf had even the smallest hint of interest in you, she'd be pushing to take over. She would be impossible to control after resisting the pull this long. Except there isn't any attraction, only disgust."

"Why do you have to be so damn stubborn?" He

raked his fingers through his hair, pacing back and forth next to my car. "If you'd just give into our mating, all of your problems would be over. Nobody would dare to give you shit anymore."

"I'm sure everyone would be thrilled with the idea of me being their future luna after the smear campaign you've done." I laughed, but it was dry and without an ounce of humor. "Even before you convinced our fellow packmates that I have no regard for fated matings, people would have been appalled by the idea of you leading this pack with me at your side."

He puffed his chest out and shook his head. "No, they'll be fine with it. I'm going to be the alpha some-day, nobody would have the nerve to cross me."

I didn't bother pointing out that I had dared to do just that, over and over again for the past few months. Elijah was too arrogant to listen to reason. Instead, I took the opportunity to slip into the driver's seat since he was near the back of my car. Then I started the engine and quickly pulled out of the parking lot.

Although my hands had been steady earlier, I had to tighten my hold on the wheel until my knuckles whitened because they were trembling now. I was furious and didn't know how much more of this crap I could take.

After spending fifteen years in this pack and never causing a single problem, it would've been nice if people judged me on my own merits instead of lumping me in with my parents. Especially now that they were gone. Except my place in the pack hadn't improved. It had only become more precarious.

The bad reputation that I'd done nothing to earn had made it easy for Elijah to single me out. I didn't know if he truly believed what he said or if he had somehow deluded himself. Either way, I couldn't continue to live under these conditions any longer. Something had to give, and I had a feeling it was going to be me because I didn't see him ever backing down after he'd dug himself in so deep.

2

JARED

I loved being my pack's beta, but I'd never been a fan of getting early morning calls even though they came with the territory. Stretching my arm, I grabbed my phone from my bedside table and answered, "Hello?"

"Good morning," Seth greeted.

I sat up at the sound of my alpha's voice. "Not sure you can call the morning good when it isn't even seven o'clock yet."

"Only because you're a night owl."

Seth had turned into a morning person when he met his fated mate. Jane worked in a tea shop and was used to getting up early, and he'd adjusted his schedule to fit hers because he'd wanted to make her adjustment to our pack as easy as possible.

I couldn't blame him for doing whatever it took to make his mate happy, but that didn't mean I felt the need to wake up before the ass crack of dawn too. Something Seth damn well knew. "Did you need something?"

"Is that any way to speak to your alpha?"

"It's absolutely how I talk to my best friend when he yanks my chain after waking me up too fucking early in the morning," I retorted, getting to my feet to stalk into my kitchen.

His laughter drifted through the line as I dropped a pod into my coffee machine and pressed the button to get it brewing. Once I was up, there was no hope of falling back asleep, but I still needed caffeine to get my day started.

"Fine, pull the best friend card."

Grabbing a mug from the cabinet, I asked, "Did you have an actual reason to call me or were you just bored and looking for someone to pester?"

"An alpha never pesters," Seth insisted with a chuckle.

I shook my head. "Did you manage to keep a straight face while you said that?"

"Nope." His tone turned serious as he added, "But if it helps, I did have a reason for waking you up. I received a request from Adan Deville, and I want to get back to him with an answer sooner rather than later."

I understood his desire to not make the demon wait any longer than necessary. Adan ranked as high in the demon world as Seth did among shifters. They didn't have a council similar to ours, but he ruled The Abyss with an iron fist that was respected by all supernatural beings. He had enough power to uphold the rules of no magic or killing at his hotel, which was why it was a popular spot. The safe harbor he provided was a hot commodity, and one people paid well for—including the shifter and witch councils since we kept him on retainer for our combined meetings.

"I'll be over in a little bit. I just need to get dressed and down some coffee first."

"Jane will have more caffeine waiting for you."

"Thanks," I murmured before gulping down my coffee.

I hung up the phone and ran a hand through my hair. Adan Deville didn't just go around making requests without good reason. This had to be important.

After quickly getting dressed, I headed out the door. When I arrived at Seth and Jane's house, she greeted me at the door with a smile. "Good morning. I have tea and scones ready if you'd like some."

"Thanks," I replied, following her into the kitchen. She poured me a cup, and I took a sip, relieved to feel the additional caffeine course through my veins even if it wasn't from coffee. I beamed a smile at my alpha's fated mate. "There was a time when I would've said that I'd never become a tea drinker, but you proved me wrong, Jane. As long as you're the one making it, I'm happy to drink it."

"You're welcome to come over for some whenever you want." She slid a cranberry orange scone on a plate and set it in front of me. "And the kitchen is always well stocked with baked goods."

"Only because I get your favorites shipped in for you every month from the same baked good club that you got Cassandra as a thank-you gift," Seth grumbled, shooting me an irritated look as he joined us in the kitchen.

"Quit being so growly." Jane stretched up to give him a quick kiss and patted his chest. "The least we can do is share with Jared when you dragged him out of bed this early in the morning."

I slathered a chunk of the scone with clotted cream and jam before shoving it into my mouth. Letting out a low hum of appreciation, I nodded.

"Consider it a baked goods surcharge for meetings at the ass crack of dawn."

Sliding his arm around Jane's back, Seth narrowed his eyes at me. "If you found yourself your own mate, maybe you'd have shit like this at your house. Then you could eat before you come over and leave my woman's treats alone."

"My treats?" Jane echoed with a roll of her eyes. "It's just a scone, Seth."

He was acting exactly how a fated mate should, so I couldn't blame him. But I could be envious as fuck. I wanted what Seth had found with Jane for myself. Being around the happy couple had made me feel the lack of my own mate even more lately.

When my chuckle over his possessiveness earned me a glare from him, I held my hands up in a gesture of surrender. "You don't have to convince me. I'd be fucking thrilled to meet my fated mate."

Seth gave me a pointed look. "How many times do I have to tell you to pull your thumb out of your ass and give Cassandra O'Clare a call?"

"Oh, yes!" Jane clapped her hands and beamed a smile at me. "Are you thinking about finally asking her for help? You really should, she is so amazing."

"Damn straight," Seth agreed, pressing a kiss to his mate's cheek. "The dragoness somehow knew

Jane and I belonged together before I even showed up to talk to her about finding my mate."

"You two were definitely lucky." My wolf grumbled in my head, unhappy about how long we'd been waiting for our mate. Remembering the conversation we'd had before he left for his meeting with the shifter matchmaker, I thought of a surefire way to divert our conversation into a different direction. "Just think, if you'd gone with my suggestion of me coming with you to see Cassandra O'Clare, we could've ended up as a throuple."

Seth's wolf flashed in his eyes, and he pulled Jane closer against his side. "Enough small talk. I called you over because there's business to discuss."

Seth was chosen to lead the shifter counsel in large part because he was so intimidating, but his grumbling had zero effect on Jane. Arching her brow, she leveled an unimpressed look his way. "If you wanted your meeting to be all about business, you shouldn't have invited our friend into our home."

"Sorry, baby. Talk all you want." He kissed her cheek again. "Just so long as you understand that I'm going to have to kick my beta's ass if he looks at you for too long after that dumbass statement."

Jane tilted her head with a laugh. "Can you

blame him for pushing your buttons after you told him to pull his head out of his butt?"

I finished off my scone with a laugh as my alpha murmured something in his mate's ear that made her blush. Then I pushed away from the counter. "Before this turns X-rated, we should probably discuss Adan's request."

"Now you're in a rush to get down to business," he muttered, Jane's giggles following us as we headed to Seth's office.

While he circled the desk and sat down, I dropped onto a chair across from him. "What did Adan want?"

"He saw a picture of a demon on a gossip site, but it turned out the guy wasn't born one of them," he explained, pulling up the story on his computer and turning the monitor so I could see the screen. "Just about everyone in this town apparently turned into monsters a few decades ago due to some kind of fuckup by a local scientist who made a drink for a Halloween party."

"Damn, that must've been hard as fuck to deal with." My eyes widened as I read the article. "At least some of the residents have managed to still find the equivalent of their fated mate."

"Except this guy fell for an author who's in the

spotlight just enough for people to post photos of her online." He tapped his finger against the screen. "And there's no hiding those horns of his."

I let out a low whistle. "They didn't just catch him at the wrong time while he was morphing between his human and demon shapes?"

Seth shook his head. "The information Adan has been able to dig up so far seems to indicate that the residents of Screaming Woods aren't as lucky as us. There's no hiding that they're monsters."

As much as I loved being in my wolf form, I couldn't imagine how much more difficult my life would've been if it was obvious that I was a wolf shifter. Humans weren't a forgiving bunch when it came to what was different. Being able to blend in had served me well.

"Is Adan worried about him drawing attention to other demons?"

"Yeah, the last thing his community needs is for people to find out their kind walks the planet with us," he confirmed with a nod.

Thinking about how powerful the demon was, I drew my brows together. "Does he want our help taking care of the problem so he doesn't run the risk of exposing himself?"

"Nope, he was looking for intel only, hoping we

had more information than he'd been able to dig up on the residents of Screaming Woods so far," he explained, strumming his fingers against the top of his desk. "I was hoping you've heard more than me since people tend to open up to you, but based on your reaction, I'm guessing not."

"I'll definitely keep my ears open, but this is the first I've heard of this town, so I don't have anything for Adan. Sorry."

3

RORY

Packing up and disappearing in the middle of the night was the last thing my inner animal wanted to do, but I didn't feel as though I had any choice. Elijah had done too good of a job over the past few months smearing what little goodwill I had within the pack. If I took the situation to his father, it was going to be a he said she said situation. There was no way for me to prove that we weren't fated to be together, and Ezra was already going to be biased in his son's favor.

I refused to complain, though, no matter how frustrated I was that I had been forced to sneak off pack land in the middle of the night. My mom had always complained about how unfair life was, even when they got into trouble of their own making.

Once I was old enough to know better, their incessant whining rubbed me the wrong way.

Not that there was anyone I could share my problems with even if I wanted to. My parents had both been only children, and their parents had passed away so long ago that I didn't even remember meeting them when I was a baby or toddler.

It wasn't until I had been on the road for five hours and the sun was starting to rise that a story my mom had shared with me many years ago popped into my head. I'd asked her why my kindergarten teacher didn't like me, and she had explained that sometimes it took people awhile to accept outsiders. Our pack was fairly closed off from the world, and we were the only new members to have joined in the past three years. She'd glossed over the reason why we'd left our previous pack, but she had explained how the alpha wolf who currently led the shifter council had been the one who sent us to our new home.

I had never met Seth Bashar, but I'd heard plenty of stories about him. From everything I'd heard about how he had helped to bring the shifter and witch communities together, he was an open-minded man. He was also the only shifter with enough authority over my alpha to make him back down from trying to force me back onto pack land. And luckily for me, his phone number was available to all shifters because he wanted to be accessible to anyone who needed him.

I kept driving until it was late enough to call without being rude. Then I pulled over to refill my gas tank for the second time and added some water to my radiator since my car was running a little hot. After I used their restroom and grabbed some snacks and a huge coffee, I got back into my car and took my phone out of my purse.

My hands trembled as I tapped against my screen to pull up the website for Kodiak, the town where Seth's pack had settled several generations ago. There was a section where you could log in to pay for a code violation that actually granted access to the shifter council website. After checking the entry in my notes app, I typed in the password that was shared by the members of our pack and clicked over to the directory. Without giving myself time to change my mind, I clicked on the number and placed the call.

I strummed my fingers against my steering wheel while I waited for him to pick up. Luckily, it only took three rings before I heard a deep voice clip out, "Seth Bashar."

My wolf recognized his dominance, even over the phone, and perked up at his greeting. Her reaction did nothing to soothe my nerves, though. "Um... hello. Sorry to bother you, but I didn't know where else to turn."

His tone was much softer as he replied, "If you're a she-wolf in need of help, then you picked the right person to call. When I was appointed to the shifter council, the well-being of every wolf shifter became my responsibility."

"Okay." My shoulders slumped in relief.

"Do you feel comfortable sharing your name with me?"

Since I was already far from home, I didn't hesitate to answer, "Uh-huh, I'm Rory Parker."

"Rory Parker?" he echoed, sounding surprised.

I had an empty feeling in the pit of my stomach, and my palms were sweaty. My nerves got the better of me as I babbled, "Yes, I'm a part of the Berge Pack. Or at least I was. I'm not sure exactly what I am now since I left last night. More like super early this morning, I guess."

"I know who you are, Rory."

"Oh." His answer surprised me. "I wasn't expecting that you'd remember me from when you helped my parents since I was just a little kid back then. It's been such a long time."

"You were memorable, even as a toddler." He chuckled softly. "Between all of the questions you asked and your big, golden eyes, you made quite the impression on me."

My lips parted on a gasp. "I didn't realize we actually met."

"I'm not surprised your memories are vague. It was a scary time for you before Trey and I located you guys."

This time it was my turn to echo him. "Trey?"

"The alpha of your former pack," he explained. "Since my pack was closest to his, he came to me for assistance when you disappeared with your parents."

I bit my bottom lip, worried that Ezra would be on the phone to him to ask for help in finding me as soon as we hung up. "Do you get calls from alphas every time a member leaves without talking to them first?"

"No, and even if Ezra does, you don't need to worry about me sharing anything with him unless you've given me your express permission or others' safety is at stake."

"I have no desire to hurt anyone, not even Elijah after all the headaches he's caused me." I didn't know who to trust, but his promise was exactly what I needed to hear at that moment and went a long way toward building my faith in him. "I didn't feel as though staying with my pack was an option for me any longer, but I don't have anywhere else to go."

"What kind of headaches?" he asked.

I gave him a quick rundown of the crap Elijah had pulled in the past few months, ever since my eighteenth birthday. I didn't go into too many details since that would've taken way too long, but the information I shared was enough to elicit a deep growl from the head of the shifter council. It also convinced him to help me.

"Come to my pack lands, and we can discuss your options."

My eyes widened in shock. "Really? Are you sure?"

"Absolutely. I have no doubt we can find a place where you feel comfortable. Maybe even here or with Trey, depending on what you need."

His certainty calmed me enough that my hands no longer shook. "I think I'm about five hours away."

"Perfect, head straight to Kodiak," he instructed with a thread of command in his tone. "I'll send you a text with my address. If I'm not at home when you arrive, my mate will be here. Don't worry, I won't be long, and she'll take great care of you until we can speak."

"Thank you." Tears welled in my eyes, and I felt lighter than I had in months. "I feel so much better now that I know where I'm headed."

We said our goodbyes, and my phone dinged with the notification for his text less than a minute later. Pulling out of the parking lot, I just hoped that my car would make it the rest of the way without breaking down. It had already been on its last legs when my dad bought the vehicle for me two years ago and wasn't ideal for a long road trip. But it and the suitcases I had tossed into the trunk were the grand total of my possessions beyond the few hundred dollars in my checking account, so I didn't have any other options.

4

JARED

"**A**re you ready to meet your fated mate?"

It took a lot to surprise me, but finding the dragoness who specialized in setting shifters up with their fated mates standing behind me in line at the grocery store was a shock. Especially since Seth had just brought her up to me yesterday.

Although I hadn't admitted it to him or Jane, I had thought about paying the matchmaker a visit many times over the past several months. My responsibilities to the pack kept getting in the way, or at least that was what I told myself. It was also possible I'd been using them as an excuse because I was afraid that she wouldn't be able to do for me what she'd accomplished so easily for my alpha.

I narrowed my eyes as I murmured, "Cassandra O'Clare, what're you doing around here?"

"That depends. Are you asking me as the beta of your pack or a potential client?" She grinned up at me. "My answer might differ depending on which hat you're wearing."

I shrugged with a smile. "Let's call it curiosity since most people don't shop five hours from home."

"Don't worry. I'm not here for some nefarious purpose. I'm just driving through Kodiak on the last leg of a road trip. I like to plan my pit stops in shifter towns because I never know when inspiration for a pairing will strike." She laughed and patted my arm. "Which brings me back to my question, which you're not going to be able to avoid answering quite that easily. Being a matchmaker requires a lot of persistence when you're dealing with shifters."

I was more than a little envious of how happy Seth was with Jane. I wanted what Cassandra had helped them find together, so there was only one answer I could give. "Yes, I'm ready to meet my fated mate."

"Good." Her eyes swirled with flames, signaling that she was accessing her dragon magic. "Because it's going to happen sooner than you expect."

The cashier called out the total for my items

while I was taking in Cassandra's response. Wondering how soon her prediction might come true, I turned to swipe my debit card in the reader. After I entered my PIN and swung back around, the matchmaker had disappeared as though she'd never been there.

"So fucking weird," I mumbled, grabbing my bags of groceries and carrying them out to my truck. I stowed them in the back of the extended cab before climbing into the driver's seat. As I was pulling out of the parking lot, Seth called my cell. Skipping over the usual greeting, I said, "You're never going to believe who I just bumped into at the store."

"Rory Parker?" he guessed.

I tapped my finger against my chin as I tried to place the name. It took me a moment to remember the request for help from the alpha of the nearest pack at least a decade ago when he had a family who disappeared in the middle of the night. Trey hadn't been overly worried about the parents because they'd been old enough to take care of themselves, but their little girl had been his to protect as her alpha. He'd felt like shit when he hadn't been able to track them down on his own.

With the pup's safety on the line, Trey hadn't allowed his pride to get in the way of asking for help.

It had turned out to be a lucky call because Jared had been the one to locate them. The parents had fallen in with a bad crowd, and it had taken the combined effort of both alphas to pull them out of the situation they'd allowed their greed to put them in. Cheating a bunch of criminals out of a bundle of cash had landed all three of them in danger—and put the existence of shifters at risk of being discovered by humans who couldn't be trusted to keep our secret.

"Why would you think I saw her?" My brows drew together. "I thought her family joined that pack up in the wilds of Oregon, far enough away from civilization that there wouldn't be opportunities for her parents to get into trouble again?"

"They did," he confirmed, "but only because I didn't give them much of a choice. Even though Karla and Daniel had royally fucked up, they loved their daughter and there was no other family to raise her. Taking Rory away from her parents wouldn't have been right, so I needed to make sure they had a safe place for her to grow up. Ezra rules the Berge Pack with an iron fist. I knew he wouldn't let them get away with any shit."

"Is she visiting by herself? Or did her parents assume that enough time had passed to show their faces around here? That'd be pretty damn ballsy.

Now that their daughter is old enough to take care of herself, you no longer have a reason to go easy on them if they fuck up again."

"There's no risk of that happening. Rory's on her own now. Her parents died a few months ago," Seth explained.

"Shit," I grunted, feeling bad for the she-wolf who'd already been through so much.

"It gets worse," he warned. "The reason she's headed this way is because of an issue with her alpha's son. She didn't know who else to turn to for help, but her parents had told her at least some of the story of how they ended up with their pack. Without anywhere else to turn, I think she figured she could trust me because of how I handled the situation back then."

It didn't matter that I had never met Rory; I didn't like the idea of some guy bothering any woman, let alone one on her own. My wolf was in agreement and wanted to hunt him down to rip his throat out. "What kind of problems?"

"He's convinced they're fated to be together, but she insists that isn't possible because she feels no pull toward him."

My eyes widened at his answer. The connection between mates was impossible to miss, and there was no mistaking it for something else. "That's fucked up."

"With his dad being the alpha, the situation is more than just uncomfortable for her. She sounded relieved by the possibility of joining our pack."

"I hope you're planning to offer her a spot," I growled, my hands clenching the steering wheel hard enough for my knuckles to whiten.

"You're my best friend and second-in-command. You should damn well know she'll be welcome here if this is where she wants to be," he snapped.

"You're right. Sorry." I ran my fingers through my hair and sighed. "I'm not sure what the fuck is wrong with my wolf today. He's on edge for some reason, and I have no clue why."

"Shit, I was going to ask you to sit in on my meeting with Rory, but maybe it's better if you stay away. With what she's going through, I wouldn't be surprised if she's skittish around males. In fact, I should probably ask her if she wants to be placed in a pack with more females than we have."

"No way." My reaction was fierce, and I shook my head even though he couldn't see me. "She called you for help, not some other alpha of a pack where you can't guarantee she'd be any better off than she was before."

"Even if I'm not her alpha, Rory's safety is important to me. It isn't just because of how I feel about a man who might try to force a mating with an unwilling woman because he thinks they're fated mates after what happened to Jane. Or even the fact that I swore to protect all wolves when I took my place on the council, either. I'm the one who placed them in that pack when she was a child," he reminded me. "If she's interested, I'm sure the Black River Pack would be happy to take her in, and Hunter is an excellent alpha."

"But you already agreed she could come here." I turned into my neighborhood, and my wolf pushed against my skin. My frustration continued to build, and I pounded my fist against the console at my side.

"To meet with me and figure out her options," he corrected. "I didn't commit to anything other than talking with Rory. I would never accept someone into our pack without getting a feel for them face-to-face first unless they mated in. Rory was sweet the last time I saw her, but she was only a toddler. I have no idea what kind of person she is now or where she'd be the happiest."

I took a few deep breaths in a failed attempt to calm down. "When are you meeting with her? I want to be there."

"Soon. She should already be in town, and I didn't want to waste any time."

Some of the tension drained from my body upon hearing she was near. "Good, I'm almost home. I'll drop my groceries off and head over to your house. It shouldn't take me more than half an hour."

"I guess I'll see you soon, then. But you never said...who did you bump into at the store?" he asked.

Turning onto my street, I answered, "Cassandra O'Clare."

"Really?"

"Yeah—" The words dried up in my throat when I pulled into my driveway and spotted the woman sitting on my front step. The gorgeous blonde with golden eyes had mouthwatering curves, and my wolf wanted out of my skin to get to her. Badly.

5

RORY

When I arrived in Kodiak, I had fully intended to head straight to the alpha's house. I didn't know anyone in his pack, but I found myself deviating from the directions my GPS gave me when I was only a few blocks away. It felt as though my wolf was urging me toward a specific location, and she didn't back down until I pulled in front of a white house with dark-blue shutters. When I got out of my car, the reason for her insistence hit me like a sledgehammer. The delicious scent surrounding the house could only belong to one person—my fated mate.

I ran from my home in the middle of the night with no destination in mind and somehow managed to stumble upon my mate's home.

His scent was just faint enough for me not to be surprised when my knock on the door went unanswered. I had no way of knowing when he'd be back, but I sat on his front step to wait him out. Although my meeting with Seth was urgent, nothing was more important than finding the man who I was fated to spend the rest of my life with.

Half an hour later, a truck pulled into the driveway. The moment the driver's gaze met mine through the windshield, I knew I was right about finding my fated mate.

My wolf pushed for control, wanting to mark him as ours to warn off other women. When he climbed out of his vehicle, his delicious scent hit me, and the fight to keep my wolf tethered in my human skin became more difficult. Not that I blamed her since the man striding toward me was sexy as heck. He was a few inches over six feet with dark-brown hair and bright-blue eyes. They flashed wolf as he stalked toward me, and my animal side tried to lunge for him again.

"Hello." My greeting turned into a gasp when he bent low and lifted me off the stoop. Taking advantage of my parted lips, my fated mate claimed my mouth without saying a word. His tongue swept inside to tangle with mine, and I twined my arms around his neck. Giving myself up to his kiss, I didn't notice that he'd gotten the front door open and carried me inside the house until he dropped me onto the mattress in his bedroom.

He quickly followed me down, bracing his hands against the mattress to hover over my body. "I'm Jared."

"And I'm Rory."

Recognition flared in his eyes before his lips brushed against mine again. "My mate."

"I found you." My fingers toyed with the hair at the back of his head, stroking his scalp.

He claimed my mouth again, kissing me until I was panting in need. "I want to know everything that brought you here, but later."

"Yes, later," I echoed in agreement, my hands drifting down to tug his shirt over his head. With his hard length pressed against my core and my wolf all riled up, my need to be mated and marked by Jared was overwhelming. It didn't take long for us to kick off our shoes and strip out of our clothes, and our greedy hands and mouths began to explore the skin we'd bared.

With his strong hands on me, I felt as though I'd been struck by lightning. Arousal spread through my veins, priming my body so I would be ready for Jared to claim me. I had never given myself to anyone else, but I didn't feel an ounce of fear. I knew my fated mate would take good care of me.

With his body levered over mine, Jared lowered his head to lick over my shoulder. "I'm going to enjoy the fuck out of marking you as mine when your tight pussy is wrapped around my cock."

My inner walls fluttered at the sensual promise in his deep voice. "Yes, please. I need you so much."

"You're going to have me, baby. Always."

My breath caught in my chest as I realized I'd never be alone again. This man would stand by my side no matter what I faced in the future.

Jared trailed hot, wet kisses along my collarbone. Arching my back off the mattress, I pressed my breasts into his palms. He cupped the weight in his hands, and my nipples pebbled. They were practically begging to be sucked into his mouth.

As though he could read my mind, Jared bent his head to circle his tongue around the puckered peak. "Please," I panted, threading my fingers through his thick hair to tug him closer.

His blue eyes locked on my face as he wrapped his lips around the tip of my breast and sucked. He toyed with that side for a minute before paying the same attention to the other. By the time he moved lower, I was already close to the edge and unsure how much more pleasure I could take before I flew apart.

Jared knelt between my legs and stared down at me, licking his lips. Then he trailed his hands up the inside of my thighs. When he reached the bare, glistening folds of my sex, he parted my lower lips with his thumbs. "So fucking gorgeous, and all mine."

He got down on his stomach again, and I widened my legs to make it easier for him to wedge his shoulders between them. Slipping his hands under my butt, he lifted me to his mouth. His breath was hot against my core as he groaned, "You smell incredible, and I bet you're going to taste even better."

My orgasm rushed over me with the first swipe of his tongue, but my cries of completion only spurred him on. He ate me through my release, licking and sucking until I was already climbing higher again. Then he started to work a finger into my core, flicking his tongue over my clit until I was slippery wet and could easily take his thick digit.

His eyes burned into mine as he murmured, "Your pussy is clamped down so hard against my finger. I can't wait to feel you wrapped around my cock like this. But I need you to let go for me again, baby. Give me another one so you'll be ready to take me."

With our gazes locked, he added another finger and stroked inside my channel. It wasn't long before I shouted his name as I came again. Once my shudders subsided, he placed a soft kiss just above my mound before lining his hard-on up with my entrance.

We stared into each other's eyes as he slowly filled me, giving me enough time to lessen the pain of losing my virginity. When he was finally anchored deep inside my pussy, he groaned, "So fucking perfect."

"Yes," I panted, my fingernails digging into his back as my legs circled his hips. "But I need you to move."

"Whatever you want, baby." He shifted his hips until his tip was at my entrance again and then inched back inside. His pace was slow at first, but he started going faster as we got closer to the edge of our control. He kept powering into me, each thrust harder than the last until my orgasm crashed over me, and I cried out his name. When my inner walls clamped down hard, he roared my name, "Rory! Fuck, yes!"

My wolf's fur itched against my skin, pushing for

the next steps in the mating process. Staring up at my gorgeous mate, I whispered, "Mate me. Mark me. I don't want to wait."

"That's good, baby. My wolf would give me hell if I let you out of this bed without my mark on your shoulder."

With his hard length anchored deep inside me, Jared uttered the words that tied us together forever.

"Ich beanspruche dich als meine Gefährtin, von jetzt an bis in alle Ewigkeit."

The connection between us was already building, but it wasn't enough. Seeing that his canines were lengthening, I tilted my head to the side so he could sink them into my shoulder. Light sparked behind my eyes, and I felt a jolt in my chest. Our bond snapped into place, triggering another orgasm as tears of relief filled my eyes.

But even that didn't settle my wolf. She wanted more.

The claiming—the final step in the shifter mating process—couldn't happen until the next full moon, but I could give her something else now. Although not all female shifters marked their mate in return, my inner beast urged me to sink my teeth into his shoulder.

Jared proved yet again that fate had been right to

pair us together. Rolling onto his back while we were still locked together, he settled me on top of his muscular body and turned his head until he'd pressed his cheek against the pillow. "Go ahead. Mark me too, baby. I'll be proud to wear your bite on my shoulder."

"Thank you." I loved that he so readily accepted what I wanted without any hesitation.

My gums ached as my canines extended. The slight pain was more than worth it when I sank them into his shoulder and felt as though I'd found a piece of my soul that I hadn't even known was missing.

Jared wrapped his hands around my waist and powered up into me. I wasn't sure if it was my pleasure or his that sent me hurtling into another orgasm —that was how in sync we already were with each other. Either way, the release was more intense than the others he'd just given me.

We rocked against each other until the shudders subsided. Then I collapsed against Jared's chest, and he stroked his hand down my spine. "Holy fuck, Rory. I've never felt anything like that."

"Neither have I," I whispered.

Pressing a finger beneath my chin, Jared tilted my head until our gazes met. "I'm so grateful for the gift you just gave me, baby. I never expected my mate to wait for me, but knowing that you did means the fucking world to me."

My cheeks filled with heat as I admitted, "I wish I could say the choice was intentional, but it was more a case of not really having many opportunities except for one I had absolutely no interest in taking."

"You're mine now." His hold on me tightened. "You don't have to worry about that dipshit alpha's son ever again. Anybody who so much as thinks about trying to take you from me will be in for a rude awakening."

My eyes widened as I realized my mate knew exactly who I was and why I'd come to Kodiak.

6

JARED

I had already been pissed on Rory's behalf when Seth had told me about her call. But knowing I never would have found and mated her if that bastard had talked her into believing his delusion sent my fury to a whole new level.

I was so angry that it took a moment to notice my mate was staring at me in confusion. Guessing the reason behind her surprise, I explained, "I was on the phone with Seth when I pulled up. He gave me a heads up on your situation because he wanted me to sit in on your meeting with him as his beta."

"You're the Kodiak Pack beta?" Rory gasped, her pretty golden eyes widening.

"And Seth's best friend," I confirmed with a nod.

"Wow." She cupped my cheek with her palm,

stroking my scruff. "I guess my alpha and his son are in for a heck of a surprise if they come looking for me."

"Damn straight." I pressed a kiss against her temple. "I'm the only mate you'll ever have."

"You won't hear any arguments from me." She rubbed her cheek against my chest. "I'll never want anyone else."

I pressed a finger under Rory's chin to tilt her head back until I could see her eyes. "Do you have any idea why the alpha's son from your previous pack tried to convince you that you were supposed to be his when you're mine and only mine?"

"My previous pack, huh?" Her lips kicked up in a teasing grin.

I nodded. "I'm Seth's beta, and you're my mate. There's no question about which pack you belong to now, baby."

She beamed a smile at me. "You make an excellent point."

"My position will be useful when the time comes to handle the wolf who tried to steal you from me." I glided my hand down her back in a soothing gesture. "Tell me what happened."

"As the alpha's son, Elijah was used to women falling into his bed with a snap of his fingers. Not me, though. I think the distance I kept people at presented a challenge to him at first. But he wasn't happy after I turned him down a few times." She buried her face in my chest and inhaled my scent deep into her lungs before she continued. "Coincidentally, rumors started going around the day after he asked me out for the third time. At first, there were whispers about how much of a whore I was, which was ironic since there wasn't a single male wolf in the pack who could honestly say I'd ever slept with him."

"Fucking bastards." I was the only man who could ever make that claim, and I wanted to rip the throat out of everyone who'd dared to spread lies about my mate.

"Then there was some crap about me being an ice-cold bitch who'd turned her fated mate away because I didn't want to be locked down until I was older. The last straw was when someone who has known me since I was three years old asked me about my arrest record yesterday. Spoiler alert: I don't have one."

My muscles were coiled for battle as I asked, "What did Ezra have to say about the shit his son was pulling?"

"Going to my alpha didn't seem like a good

option. Elijah was sneaky in his whisper campaign. He never directly hurt or threatened me, and I couldn't find proof that he was behind the rumors." She rubbed her cheek against my chest again and yawned. "That's why I decided to leave."

"Don't worry, sweetheart." I combed my fingers through her hair. "That's all behind you now."

After running scared in the middle of the night, Rory had been mated, marked, and fucked to within an inch of her life. She had probably already been exhausted before I completely wore her out. I wasn't surprised that she drifted off to sleep while I held her.

I was thrilled that my mate felt safe enough to finally rest, but I needed to get a handle on the situation with her former pack. The last thing I wanted was for her to be in any kind of danger, even though I had the utmost confidence in my ability to protect her.

Enjoying the feel of Rory's naked body sprawled against mine, I held her until someone pounded on the front door. Not wanting the sound to wake her, I left my gorgeous mate sleeping in my bed while I yanked on a pair of jeans. Ready to kick some ass over the interruption that pulled me away from Rory so soon after our mating, I stormed down the stairs and flung open the door.

"You hung up on me." Seth's grin made it clear he wasn't pissed about it, though.

I leaned against the door frame and crossed my arms. My alpha was mated, but I didn't want another guy in my house while Rory was naked. "That was hours ago, and you're just now checking on me? I could've been dead in a ditch for all you knew."

"Nah, one of your neighbors saw you haul a woman into your house around the same time. I put two and two together and came up with a theory." His gaze dropped to the bite mark Rory had left on my shoulder. "And it looks like I was right. You found your mate."

"I can't claim the credit for finding her when she's the one who showed up on my doorstep instead of heading to your house," I corrected.

Catching onto what I was hinting at, Seth's dark eyes widened. "Rory is your mate?"

"She is," I confirmed with a shit-eating grin. "Now the little bastard giving her a hard time can back the fuck off or answer to me."

"I have a feeling he's not going to back off without a fight." Seth rubbed his hand down his face. "Ezra called to request a meeting about an issue with

Rory. Since I was the one who asked him to take her family in, he thought I should know that she disappeared last night after causing trouble in his pack."

"You have to be fucking kidding me." My fists clenched as I straightened. "She didn't cause shit. His son spread a fuck ton of rumors about her because he wanted to alienate my mate and make her even more vulnerable than she already was."

"You don't have to convince me of her innocence," he reassured, glancing over my shoulder with a sigh. "Even if I hadn't already heard the fear in her voice for myself when she called this morning, all it would take was one word from you for me to be on her side. You've more than earned my trust, and I know how strong the mating bond is, even when it's brand new. You'd know if she wasn't telling the truth."

I hadn't doubted that Seth would have my back— and Rory's as my mate—but hearing him confirm it appeased my wolf a little. "What kind of alpha goes running to the head of the shifter council because his son wants a woman who doesn't belong to him?"

"One who won't hold his position much longer," he muttered with a fierce scowl.

My nostrils flared as I huffed out a breath. "Too bad I have no interest in leading a pack of my own.

I'm more than tempted to issue the bastard a challenge after I take care of his son."

"Let's not jump straight to killing anyone," Seth suggested, shaking his head as he chuckled.

"That's easy for you to say," I grumbled as I narrowed my eyes at him. "There isn't some asshole out there trying to lay claim to Jane."

"There damn well better not be." His wolf flashed in his eyes, and alpha waves blasted into the room.

As his beta, I was able to withstand his show of dominance to a certain extent. Crossing my arms over my chest, I quirked my brow. "See, you'd be ready to kill someone too."

"I would," he conceded, pinching the bridge of his nose. "But I'm going to have to ask you to exercise the same restraint I would be forced to have. As head of the shifter council, I'm held to a higher standard. And so are you, as my beta."

"Motherfucker," I bit out, pacing back and forth while I wrestled with the unfortunate fact that he was right. Fated mates were sacred, but taking out the alpha of another pack came with political ramifications that could cause all sorts of trouble when all I wanted was to start building my life with Rory. "Keep the bastard away from my mate, and I might be able to convince my wolf not to rip his throat out."

"That's good enough for me." He clapped me on the back and turned to head down the steps. When he reached the bottom, he looked over his shoulder. "Let your mate know I'm looking forward to welcoming her to our pack whenever you're ready to share her with anyone."

I slammed the door shut, and his laughter drifted through the hard surface as I stalked back to the bedroom. Rory had woken up while I was gone and put her shirt and panties back on. It was a damn good thing that Seth wasn't expecting to see us anytime soon. Knowing that I'd have my beautiful mate all to myself for a little while eased some of my irritation at him for interrupting her rest.

7

RORY

My reprieve from meeting with Seth only lasted two days. Jared and I spent just about every hour in bed together, except for when we let our wolves out for a run so they could have time with each other. I was happier than I'd ever been...at least until Jared received a text from Seth while we were eating breakfast.

"Seth heard from your former alpha again. He wants us to come over today."

My stomach turned, so I pushed my plate away. "When?"

Attuned to me in a way that only mates could be, Jared jerked his head up. His eyes narrowed as he scanned my face. "Don't worry, baby. It sucks that we have to deal with this bullshit, but Seth and Jane are looking forward to finally meeting you. They won't do anything to make you uncomfortable."

It was difficult to wrap my head around the fact that the head of the shifter council was now my alpha—and my mate's best friend. I was going to see one of the most powerful shifters just about every day for the rest of my life. Starting today.

Standing with a sigh, I mumbled, "I guess we should get this over with."

Shaking his head, Jared shoved the last bite of his waffle into his mouth and snatched my plate before I could pick it up. Getting to his feet, he finished off the rest of my bacon. Then he rinsed everything off and loaded them into the dishwasher while I wiped down the counters.

"Ready to go?"

Sliding my hands up his chest, I blinked up at him. "Any chance I can talk you into heading upstairs to hide in bed with me instead?"

"After we get this meeting out of the way, sure."

"Drat," I huffed.

Chuckling, he kissed the tip of my nose. "You're so fucking cute, baby. Even when you're flustered for no reason."

Butterflies swirled in my belly over how sweet this strong beta wolf was with me. "I really hope you're right, but my experiences with wolves who've gotten a taste of power isn't all that great."

His expression turned serious, and his wolf flashed in his eyes. "Elijah never should've gotten away with the bullshit he pulled. Any alpha who deserves his position protects the wolves who choose to follow him and trains those who lead beside him to value each and every member of their pack. Seth and I learned that lesson from his father when we were young."

The mating bond allowed me to understand Jared on a deep level in a very short amount of time. I already knew he was loyal to a fault and not just to his alpha. He took his beta duties seriously and was a protector to his core. Although I was nervous to meet Seth, I trusted my mate's judgment. He wouldn't choose to lead beside someone who hadn't earned his respect.

"As long as I have you by my side, I know I'll be fine."

"Better than fine, baby," he growled, wrapping his fingers around my wrist to yank me against his chest. "You deserve the very best, and that's what I'll make sure you get. Always, because that's how long I'll be by your side."

"Then let's do this." I interlaced our fingers. "Together."

He lifted our hands to brush a kiss against my knuckles before we headed out the door. Since it was a beautiful day, we walked the few blocks to Seth's home. Before Jared could knock on the door, it was flung open and a brunette practically threw herself toward me. "I'm so happy to meet you."

Jared steadied me with a strong hand at my lower back while I hugged the woman who I assumed was my new luna.

"You didn't even let them inside the house before you tackled the poor woman, Jane," a deep voice chided behind her. I looked over her shoulder, and the powerful man who was my new alpha smiled at me. "Sorry about that."

Jane stepped back and turned to face him, planting her hands on her hips. "I didn't tackle Rory. I hugged her."

"More like tackle-hugged," Jared corrected with a laugh.

I grinned up at my mate, completely at ease now that the ice had been broken. "Which was the best welcome I could've gotten."

"I see how it's going to be around here." Seth pulled Jane against his side and gestured for us to enter their home. "The two of you are going to team up against us, women versus men. Won't you?"

"It's only fair since I've had to put up with the two of you and your male bonding for all this time."

Her complaint made me giggle, and I sensed Jared's relief as he led me inside. Seth shut the door, and we followed them into the kitchen, where Jane poured us some tea and served delicious blueberry muffins.

When we were seated at the table, Seth said, "I'm sorry to interrupt your time together so soon after your mating, but Ezra called again. He asked for my assistance locating you, and I told him that I was dealing with an issue with the demons but would follow up with him soon. He was already getting impatient, so I don't think I'll be able to stall him much longer."

My muscles locked as I heaved a deep sigh. "I'm not sure why Elijah was so keen for me to be his fated mate in the first place. It's not as though I bring anything to the table other than myself. We were banished to his father's pack, but my parents didn't really learn their lesson and still caused all sorts of trouble. And then he trashed my reputation, which only lowered my position in the pack to a whole new level."

"You need to give yourself more credit." Pressing his finger beneath my chin, Jared tilted my head back until I met his gaze. "You don't need to bring anything else to the table. Being able to have you is more than enough."

I loved that he thought that, but he was definitely biased as my mate. "Except you kind of have to believe that because we're actually fated to be together, but the same isn't true for Elijah."

"Damn straight, it isn't," he growled, his wolf staring out at me from his deep blue eyes. "You're not his; you're mine. Only mine."

"It doesn't matter what shit Ezra tries to pull. His son won't have the chance to try to take your mate from you," Seth assured.

"What's with guys trying to pressure women to mate with them?" Jane grumbled. "I would've hoped that crap would've been put to an end after all the crap I went through with John and the lives that were lost back then."

My eyes widened as I stared at Jane. "Some guy tried to force you into a mating, too?"

She nodded. "Yes, but at least he didn't think we were actually fated to be together. Elijah has taken his pursuit of you to a different level."

A deep growl rumbled up Seth's chest. "Not sure

I can agree with you on this, baby. Don't get me wrong, the shit Elijah has pulled is awful, but he didn't get her shunned."

Shunnings were our most extreme form of punishment and almost unheard of in the shifter world. My sense of loneliness before I found Jared paled compared to what a shunned wolf experienced. They were cast out from their pack, any memories of them wiped away so that it was as though they never existed. There was no contact with family or former friends, and being accepted into another pack with that stain on your honor was virtually impossible.

I hated that Jane had gone through something so awful, but I felt an odd sense of kinship knowing she understood the depth of fear I'd felt over Elijah's antics. Reaching out, I patted her hand. "I'm so sorry."

She waved off my concern. "John is long since dead, and I'm deliriously happy now. Just like I know you'll be with Jared."

"Damn straight." My mate slid his arm around my back to give me a reassuring squeeze.

Seth nodded. "There isn't anything Ezra or Elijah can do to you. You're a member of my pack now, mated and marked by my beta."

"Let them come," Jared grunted. "I'd be more than happy to kill both assholes and be done with this whole mess."

Seth shook his head with a sigh. "No killing unless it's necessary, remember?"

"If that bastard doesn't back off my mate, my wolf won't be satisfied with anything else," Jared warned.

I cuddled into his side and rubbed my cheek against his arm, hoping to soothe my mate and his wolf. "Elijah was a horrible pest, but he's really just a guy who thinks the world owes him whatever he wants. He's a boy trying to be a man while you're a beta who's earned his place at the side of the alpha who leads the shifter council. Even if they come, he won't be able to stand up to you."

"Not many would," Seth agreed. "Ezra has been the alpha of his pack for a long time, but I have no doubt you'd be able to take him in a fight. Not that it will come to that once I have a word with him about his son's appalling behavior."

"I have no doubt you two have this situation handled, no matter what." Jane bounced on her seat and clapped her hands. "Which is why we should focus on happier things...like Jared and Rory's claiming ceremony."

8

JARED

With all of the upheaval Rory had gone through over the past few months, I hadn't expected her to be prepared for our claiming ceremony less than a week after we met. I'd been hesitant to mention that the next full moon was so soon, but it turned out that I'd been worried for nothing. I had been proud as fuck of my girl when she'd announced she was organizing our celebration with Jane, and I'd better show up if I knew what was good for me. Which I sure as hell did.

Rory was the best thing that had ever happened to me, and I would spend the rest of my life proving to her that fate hadn't fucked up by giving her to me. She had spent too many years taking other people's shit, but now she had me to ensure she got what she deserved—down to every detail she wanted for our claiming ceremony.

"Do you think you got enough flowers?" Seth shook his head with a laugh. "Those fuckers are huge."

I hadn't realized how big the lupines were until the delivery arrived a few minutes ago, but I wouldn't admit that to him. "You can make fun of me all you want, but we both know you would've done the same damn thing for Jane if she wanted them."

"Of course I would."

"Good answer," Jane drawled from behind us.

I turned to look at her, but my attention was captured by the vision of my mate in her flowing white dress standing next to her. "Holy fuck."

Jane beamed a smile at Rory. "See, I told you he'd be at a loss for words when he saw you."

"How could I not be?" I murmured, moving close to hand her the bouquet of purple flowers. "You're even more beautiful than when you left me this morning, baby."

"You're not too shabby yourself." Rory's cheeks pinkened as she lifted the flowers to her nose and sniffed them. "And these are perfect, exactly what I pictured."

"They'd better be." It took me too many phone

calls to find a florist who promised they'd be able to deliver what my mate had described to me when I'd asked her about her dream claiming ceremony. Impatient to solidify our mating with the step that would tie our wolves together forever, I pulled her against my side and turned to Seth. "Are you ready to perform the ceremony?"

"Impatient much?"

Jane walked over and elbowed him in the side. "No teasing Jared on their special day."

"Okay, baby." Seth's expression turned serious, and he nodded. "My part is easy. You and your parents already did all the hard work."

Taking that as a yes, I led Rory to the circle formed by our pack members. My parents were near where Seth would stand, and my mom rushed over to hug us. "Look at you two, such a perfect pair. I can hardly wait to see the gorgeous grandbabies you'll give me."

"Mom," I groaned, aiming a look at my dad so that he'd come get her. I appreciated that she was happy for us and welcomed Rory into our family with open arms, but I didn't need her to put any pressure on my mate while she was still adjusting to the recent changes.

Rory giggled as my dad dragged my mom away,

and the tension eased from my shoulders. Sliding my arm around her back, I turned us to face Seth. My best friend took the hint and dove straight into the words that would bless our mating, the same as I'd done for him back when he'd found Jane.

"*Seinen Gefährten zu finden ist ein Geschenk. Ich bin glücklich die Verbindung meines Bruders heute segnen zu dürfen.*"

The pack members circling us repeated the blessing, and heat streaked through my body as my wolf howled in triumph in my head. Desire coursed through my veins, and I was nearly mindless with need when I took Rory's bouquet from her hands and handed it to Jane. Knowing what came next, my mate was already streaking toward the woods before I urged, "Run."

I barely held onto my self-control during the two-minute head start I was supposed to give her, and then I was chasing after Rory. She was fast, but I was determined to catch her. It only took about five minutes for me to close the distance between us. Our animals pushed us during the claiming, and it was common for members of the pack to bear witness to the final stage of the mating. However, there was no fucking way anyone was going to see my mate when I made her come. Tossing her over my shoulder, I stalked toward the path that led to our house and carried her to our bedroom, where I had her all to myself.

After I kicked the door shut behind us, I set Rory onto her feet and took her mouth in a deep, consuming kiss. We were both panting when I lifted my head and growled, "My wolf and I are complete in a way I never expected. It's as though you smashed both sides of my soul together until we became one."

Her golden eyes were heated as she stared up at me in awe. "But better because there are parts of you interwoven throughout, too."

"Yes, that's it exactly." My wolf howled his agreement in my head, and she nodded as if the sound echoed around the room. The claiming ceremony had deepened the bond between our wolves to the point they were in sync with each other even when we were in our human forms.

"I hope you're ready for me to take you hard and fast, baby." I led her over to the bed, kicking my shoes off on the way. "I'm barely hanging on, and my wolf is pushing me to drive inside you until I'm fully sheathed by your tight, hot pussy, so I can fuck you until we both pass out."

"I'm more than ready." She slid off her heels

before stroking her hands up my chest. Then she tugged on my shirt and yanked me down to press a hard kiss against my lips. "My wolf is riding me just as hard as yours."

I loved that my mate felt comfortable enough with me to be demanding in bed. How she didn't try to hide that she wanted me. Her passion was such a turn-on, but I needed to remember how new she was to all this. "You're going to get every inch of me, but first, I'm going to lick your pussy until it's soaked enough to take me with one thrust."

My finger traced over the bodice of her dress before dipping inside to brush over one of her puckered nipples. Rory gasped and arched her back, pressing the rounded globe against my hand. "Please."

The scent of her need filled the air as I fisted the front of her dress and yanked it down, ripping the soft material until it hung in tatters from her waist. The top had been tight enough that she hadn't worn a bra, and her bare tits practically begged for attention.

Rory moaned when I bent to take a pebbled peak into my mouth. Toying with her perfect breasts, I drove her mindless with need before I spread her out on the mattress. Then I tugged what remained of her dress from her luscious body and quickly stripped out of my clothes.

Staring down at her, I took in every bared inch of her flesh. Only a pair of white lace panties blocked my view of her pretty pussy, and I tore it away just as quickly as the rest. She was drenched with need, making my mouth water. I dragged the sweet scent of her desire into my lungs, and the last of my control evaporated.

Crawling between her legs, I licked up the center of her pussy. Her sweet and spicy flavor exploded on my tongue, making me want more. With my thumbs, I gently parted her lips to lap up her cream, avoiding her clit until she begged me for release.

"Please, Jared. I'm so close," she whimpered, her nails digging into my shoulders with enough bite to let me know her wolf was close to the surface.

I lifted my gaze to meet hers. "That's right. Come for me, baby."

She let out a breathy sigh of appreciation when I finally sucked on her clit. Her nails dragged up my neck to dig into my scalp, and she held me in place as her hips lifted off the mattress. I kept at her with my mouth as I sank a finger into her snug channel, working her into a frenzy of need.

Her cries of pleasure echoed around the room as I ate at her like a starving man until she teetered at the edge of her release. I thrust a second finger inside her and scraped my teeth against her clit, tumbling her headfirst into an orgasm. "Jared, yes! Oh yes!"

Her entire body shuddered as her pussy clamped down on my fingers. Twisting my wrist, I stroked her G-spot to lengthen her release. Just as she started to come back down, I moved up her body to cover her. Her hands moved to my biceps, and her legs wrapped around my waist. My cock slipped through her wetness, and I gave in to my overwhelming need to take my mate.

I was acting on pure instinct when I shoved inside her tightness, going balls deep with one brutal thrust. "Your pussy takes me so fucking good, baby."

Her golden eyes were glossy with passion as she blinked up at me. "Because I was made for you, Jared."

"Mine," I grunted, grabbing her wrists and locking them over her head in an unyielding grip. She didn't resist, only tightening her hips around my waist to hold on while I slammed in and out of her tight pussy. Over and over again until we were both close to the edge of release.

Rory threw her head back and cried out as she

met me thrust for thrust. Her inner walls spasmed around my dick, and I knew she couldn't hold out much longer. Neither was I since my body shook from the effort to make sure she came with me.

"So close," she panted.

"Come on my cock, baby. I want to feel your pussy strangling me until I fill you with my seed."

Pressing my knees into the mattress, I hiked her hips higher to change the angle of my cock so my hard length dragged against her G-spot on my next plunge into her depths. It was exactly what Rory needed to fly apart.

"Jared! Yesss!"

"Rory!" I roared her name as I followed her into the orgasmic abyss. My hips moved with shallow pumps until our shudders subsided.

My head dropped to the crook of her neck, and I licked over the bite that marked her as mine. "Whoa, that was...incredible."

"It was perfect." Lowering my head, I kissed her with all the love that was already building inside me. "Because you're perfect for me, and our bond is unbreakable now."

9

RORY

Finding Jared had brought me so much more than just my fated mate. I was finally a welcome member of a pack, I had in-laws who showered me with all the loving care my parents had never given me, and my wolf was at peace in a way she'd never been before.

I couldn't remember the last time I had looked forward to a pack run, but I was practically vibrating with excitement as we got ready to meet everyone in the forest behind Seth and Jane's house. Normally, the run would have been last night during the full moon, but they'd wanted to focus on honoring Jared and me—even after we'd disappeared to have our own private celebration of our claiming.

"All set?" Jared asked as he padded out of our

bedroom, his jeans hanging low on his hips since the snap was undone at the top.

I bounced on the balls of my feet with a nod, a huge smile splitting my cheeks. "Uh-huh."

"Get used to being this happy all the time, baby." He stroked his thumb across my cheek. "I'm going to do whatever it takes to keep this glow on your pretty face."

"You don't need to do anything except be yourself." I twined my arms around his neck and went up on my toes to kiss him. "Being with you already puts me over the moon with happiness."

"Be careful, baby. If you keep saying sweet shit like that, we'll be late to the pack run. And Seth doesn't wait for anyone except his mate," he warned, his eyes darkening with desire.

"How much time do we have?"

He slid his hand down my spine, sending a delicious shiver in its wake. "About ten minutes, which isn't nearly long enough for me to properly enjoy your delectable body."

"Then I guess we'd better get moving." If we were leaving for anything other than my first official run with my new pack, I would have given in to the temptation of finding out how late I could make us.

"Especially since I want a few minutes with your wolf first."

We'd been so wrapped up in each other last night that our animals hadn't gotten the chance to come out, and my wolf was beyond ready to play with her mate.

Jared beamed an approving smile at me. "My wolf would love that, baby. But I'll want some time with my pretty she-wolf after the run."

My wolf's fur brushed against my skin. "Sounds like the perfect plan to me," I agreed.

Walking out to the back porch, I stared in appreciation as Jared shoved his jeans down his muscular thighs. Since he'd gone commando, his thick cock sprung free.

There was a bead of pre-come at the tip, and I licked my lips, almost tasting it on my tongue. A low groan rumbled up his chest. "You have no idea how much I wish we had more time before the run so you could fulfill the sensual promise in those sexy eyes of yours."

We'd done plenty of exploring in bed with each other, but I hadn't given him a blow job yet. "Are you finally going to let me suck you off until you lose control?"

"Yes," he hissed. "And then I'm going to drive

you wild with my mouth and fingers before I fuck the shit out of you. Including your ass since I should be able to last longer after you drain my cock with your pretty little mouth."

"Hurry up and shift," I urged, my inner walls fluttering at the hot picture he'd painted with his words. "The earlier we get this run over with, the sooner we'll get to the orgasming part of our night."

Picking up his jeans to toss them over the back of a chair, he asked, "Have I mentioned how much I like how your brain works?"

"You've been more than clear that you like everything about me."

"Not like." He lowered his head to whisper against my lips. "Love."

I'd felt the depth of his feelings for me through our mating bond, but hearing that four-letter word still stunned me. "Love?" I echoed softly.

"How could I not love you, Rory? Not only are you the perfect match for my wolf, but you're also everything I ever wanted in a mate. You're kind to people who don't even deserve your generosity and so damn sweet to me." His lips curved into a wicked grin. "And it doesn't hurt that you're seriously gorgeous and fucking fantastic in bed."

"Right back at you with that last part," I teased, my heart full to bursting.

"I'm going to need the words too, baby."

"I love you so much, Jared Oaks." Happy tears welled in my eyes. "My path to you wasn't the easiest, but every moment of worry was more than worth it because I got you in the end."

"And now my wolf and I will be around to smooth the way for you, so the rest of your days will be easier."

Flashing him a grateful smile, I watched as he transformed into his wolf. The process was quick as he changed from the sexy man I loved into a large gray wolf with the same blue eyes. "Hey there, gorgeous."

He came to me and rubbed along my legs, his fur soft against my skin. Crouching low, I rubbed my hands along the length of his body until he tilted his head and barked at me. Figuring we had run out of time before the pack run, I pulled my loose dress over my head. Then I reached for my inner wolf and gave her free rein.

I was on all fours in a flash and had to look up a little to meet Jared's gaze. He gave my nose a quick lick before bumping my side playfully. Then he leaped off the porch and raced toward the woods behind the backyard. I chased after him, and it only took a couple of minutes to reach the clearing near Seth and Jane's home. About twenty wolves waited for us, and everyone howled along with the biggest wolf when he lifted his head and bayed a welcome.

Jared and I joined in the chorus of howls, and the sound of my wolf's voice intermingling with so many others filled my heart with joy. My happiness only grew as we raced through the forest together, Jared sticking close to my side since I wasn't familiar with the territory yet. He and Seth watched over us while Jane and I romped together in our wolf forms, chasing each other through a field of dandelions.

We were both panting from exertion when we headed back into town. My wolf got a second wind when we split off from everyone to take the path that led back to our house. Knowing she would get Jared's full attention, she picked up the pace until we loped onto the back porch. Then she tilted her head and stared up at him, wagging her tail.

Jared gave me another lick on the nose and a quick nip on my shoulder before changing to his human form. Squatting down to my wolf's level, he stroked her fur while she let out sighs of utter contentment that sounded awfully close to purring. His fingers dug into my muscles, loosening knots from the run and easing aches I didn't even realize I'd had.

Giving me a final pat, he murmured, "C'mon, baby. Change back so we can head upstairs for a nice hot shower. I can hardly wait to see you on your knees in front of me with those pretty lips wrapped around my cock, and we have to get cleaned up before that can happen."

My wolf wasn't happy for her time with him to end, but she relinquished control when I pushed for it. As soon as my transformation was complete, I got to my feet and pressed my naked body against Jared's. Wrapping my hand around his hard-on, I licked my lips as I stared up at him. "Maybe my first blow job can happen in the shower, multitasking at its finest."

"It sure as fuck can, baby." Scooping me into his arms, he stalked into the house and directly up to the en suite bathroom. It wasn't long before I discovered how enjoyable it was to have my lips wrapped around his dick until he lost all control while steam swirled around us. And then I felt even more claimed when I experienced anal sex for the first time, too.

10

JARED

S eth had correctly predicted that Ezra wouldn't be put off much longer. The morning after the pack run, he showed up in Kodiak to meet with Seth. Since he'd known me all my life, he figured that the longer I had to think about the meeting, the more pissed off I would be. My anger would make it more difficult to keep myself under control, and nothing made me more furious than the thought of someone fucking with Rory.

"Since you weren't answering your phone, I came over to let you know the meeting is in five minutes at my house. I figured you'd want to be there."

"Damn straight," I agreed.

Seth was probably wise to wait until this close to

the meeting with the alpha of the Berge Pack to show up on my doorstep and give me a heads-up about it. But that didn't make me any happier that he'd pulled me away from my naked mate, who was waiting for me in bed again.

"You have the worst damn timing," I growled.

"I didn't set the meeting time. Ezra did." He shrugged with a grin. "And it's not even that early. The sun is already up."

"Yeah, but I like lazy mornings in bed even more now that I can spend them with Rory," I grumbled.

"There will be plenty of those in your future once we put this whole mess behind us."

"There better be," I grumbled, running my fingers through my hair.

"Do me a favor and get dressed before you hop in your truck. If his son shows up too and you end up kicking his ass in human form, I don't want to see you fighting in nothing but your boxers. It'd be too damn weird." He waved his hand in a downward gesture before turning around to stalk down the steps.

With no time to lose, I slammed the door shut and raced upstairs. When I strode into the bedroom, Rory sat up. The sheet fell to her hips, baring her perfect breasts. I forced my gaze up to meet her eyes because I knew we'd never make it to Seth's house before the meeting if I climbed into bed with my sexy mate. "We need to go. Ezra is on his way here to talk to Seth about the supposed problem he's having with you."

"Now?" she gasped, pointing at her chest and drawing my attention back to her tits.

I stepped into my jeans and grabbed a shirt. "Yeah."

"I guess there's no time like the present to deal with my old pack," she grumbled, scrambling for her clothes.

We hurried out to my truck, and I remembered groceries were in the back of the extended cab when the stench hit my nose. "Shit, I was so blindsided by seeing you on my front step that first day that I forgot I had stuff that needed to go into the fridge and freezer."

"Aw, I'm sorry your groceries are spoiled." Rory leaned over the console and pressed a kiss to my cheek. "But I like knowing I have the power to wipe all rational thought from your brain."

I laced my fingers through hers after I backed the truck out of my driveway. "Do me a favor and try to keep a lid on your ability. I'm already having a difficult time thinking clearly with my wolf pushing me to rip Elijah's throat out."

"I'll try, but I can't make any promises," she teased, squeezing my hand. "Not when my wolf thinks we should help with the whole ripping-the-throat-out thing now that I don't answer to his father anymore."

My dick flexed against my zipper. "Maybe start by toning down the stone-cold killer vibe because it's sexy as fuck."

"You find the oddest things sexy." She laughed and shook her head. "Then again, so do I. I guess it's another example of how we're perfect for each other."

The humor drained away when we arrived at Seth's house and discovered Ezra was already there, with Elijah at his side. My wolf was close to the surface, furious over the way Elijah's gaze remained on Rory as she climbed out of the truck. A deep growl rumbled up my chest as we walked hand-in-hand toward the front porch. I wasn't surprised that Seth hadn't invited them inside. He was standing in front of his door with his arms crossed over his chest, unwilling to run the risk of a fight breaking out anywhere near Jane.

I jerked my chin at him in greeting as I led my

mate up the steps, ignoring our visitors until we crossed the porch and were standing next to Seth. Rory was in the safest position possible with my alpha on one side and me on the other, but neither my wolf nor I were happy about her being near the guy who'd dared to mess with her.

Elijah glared at me and asked, "What's she doing here with him?"

"You're not much of a shifter if you can't tell why Rory is sticking close to Jared." Seth's taunt didn't appear to penetrate the dimwit's thick skull. "Use your shifter sense of smell or open your damn eyes, for fuck's sake."

Elijah's nostrils flared, and stunned recognition filled his eyes. "What did you do? Mate the first guy who offered after you tucked your tail between your legs and ran off?"

He proved he was dumber than I thought when he dared to take a step toward Rory. I shifted forward and to the side to block his view of her. "You'd better back the fuck up."

"There's no need to threaten my son," Ezra growled. "I came here in good faith to ask for advice from the head of the shifter council."

"I don't give a fuck if he's your son." My gaze never moved from Elijah. "Who your father is means nothing in the hierarchy of a pack until you prove you're worthy to step in his footsteps."

"As if that's ever going to happen," Rory snorted.

Elijah tried to dart around me, but I shoved him back. "You'll have to go through me to get to my mate."

His chest puffed up. "Like that'll be a problem."

"It isn't by chance that I serve as second-in-command to an alpha who heads the shifter council. My wolf's dominance and ability to fight are two of the reasons Seth chose me as his beta." I looked at Ezra. "You may want to have a chat with your son about biting off more than he can chew. After the shit he tried to pull with Rory, I won't go easy on him."

Startled awareness filled his eyes, and he reached out to yank Elijah back. "What is he talking about, son? Were you behind the rumors? Is that why nobody would tell me who started them? They were afraid to tell me my son was causing all the trouble? Not Rory?"

His reaction gave me hope that his pack wasn't as bad off as I'd originally feared. Maybe he was just an alpha with a shitty son. Then Seth wouldn't have to make sure he was challenged by someone better suited to lead his pack.

On the other hand, Elijah continued to prove how badly his throat needed to be ripped out. "What? Her parents were trash, and she should've been grateful for my attention."

There was a whisper of movement behind me, and I'd fought by Seth's side enough times to recognize he was moving closer to protect Rory. "You're the one who should be grateful. You're damn lucky to still be breathing."

"Whatever," he scoffed. "You can have her. She's not worth the trouble."

"At least you're half right. Not that I need your permission to have Rory since she's my fated mate." I strode forward, and my hand whipped out to fist the collar of Elijah's shirt. "But the part you're half wrong about is what you'll end up paying for. My mate owes you nothing, and she sure as fuck is worth the small amount of effort it will take to give you a well-earned lesson."

11

RORY

Watching Jared exact his pound of flesh from Elijah without bothering to shift into wolf form was a major turn-on. So many times, I wished I could beat the crap out of him when he was causing me trouble. Each strike of Jared's fist felt like vindication for me.

When he punched him in the nose, I remembered how often people would look down at me because he'd convinced them that I enjoyed sleeping around so much that I wanted to abandon my fated mate. With every blow, I let go of another bad memory until there weren't any left.

I was more than a little sad when it ended too quickly, though. For a guy who'd been certain he could take on my mate, Elijah gave up faster than I'd expected. Not that I blamed him since Jared had more than demonstrated why he was fit to serve as beta to the head of the shifter council by breaking his nose, right arm, and left kneecap in the first minute of the fight.

With the former bane of my existence cowering before him, Jared growled, "I want to hear you finally tell the truth. Rory isn't your fated mate. No matter how many people you lied to in an attempt to force her into accepting you, she's mine. Always has been and always will be."

Elijah spat blood on the ground with a groan. His voice was weak when he admitted, "Okay, yes...I lied. Rory isn't my mate. She's yours."

"Seriously, Elijah? How could you have fucked things up this badly?" Ezra muttered as he helped his son stand.

My guess was crappy parenting, but I decided not to say it aloud when the tension was finally easing off.

Elijah's head hung low as he admitted, "I found my mate a few months ago, but she was human and happily married with a new baby. Not being able to have her enraged my wolf, and I figured finding him a new mate would settle him down so he was easier to control."

"That fucking sucks." Jared moved to my side and wrapped his arm around my shoulders. "But there's no excuse for the shit you pulled."

With an arm braced around Elijah's back, Ezra met my eyes and lowered his head in a gesture of submission unheard of from an alpha. "I'm sorry my son created trouble for you in my pack."

"Don't worry about it on my account." I felt Jared's shock at my response and grinned. After hearing what Elijah had to say for himself and seeing my mate beat him, I knew I'd more than come out on top. "I ended up with my fated mate and an awesome pack, so I'm happy with how things turned out."

Jared brushed a kiss against my temple. "We would've found each other without him making your life miserable."

"Don't let your son ruin what you've built. Fix shit in your pack, or I'll have to send an enforcer down there," Seth warned.

"Will do," Ezra agreed before hauling Elijah down to his car and laying him out on the back seat.

I waited until they pulled away from the curb,

and then I heaved a deep sigh. I didn't enjoy talking about my life before finding Jared, but I didn't have much choice under the circumstances. "He wasn't wrong about my parents. I didn't find out about their trouble when Seth relocated us to Ezra's pack until after they died since they were always vague about what sent us there."

Jared led me inside and over to the chairs, sitting down before pulling me onto his lap. Seth dropped down on the seat next to us. "I feel as though I let you down. I shouldn't have trusted that you'd be okay in Ezra's pack. I should have checked in on you over the years, especially since I knew the kind of trouble your parents had found themselves in back then."

"It's not your fault." I beamed him a watery smile. "My parents loved me in their own way."

"Don't ever doubt that," Seth urged. "Their love for you was the only reason I sent you with them to Ezra's pack."

Jared's arms tightened around me. "It's impossible not to love you."

"Yeah, well, don't get me wrong. They still found plenty of ways to mess up, even in the middle of nowhere." I pressed my hand against my chest, feeling their loss again. "They pulled a few scams over the years, and I'm sure there were a ton more I was kept in the dark about once my parents got it through their thick skulls that I didn't want anything to do with that crap. I had already started distancing myself from them when I turned seventeen, counting down the days until I was old enough to be on my own. Then they died before my next birthday, and things got worse with the crap Elijah was pulling."

"Damn." Seth stood and paced in front of us. "I really am going to have to send an enforcer to check out what's happening with Ezra's pack. He should've come to me about all of this years ago."

"My parents were very good at keeping information to themselves. I'm not sure he even knew about that," I suggested.

"As their alpha, he damn well should have."

I felt Jared nod in agreement.

I cringed as I admitted, "If he'd gone to you, I might have gotten in trouble with the council."

"I have a well-earned reputation for being a hard-ass, but your mate can vouch for the fact that I don't judge people by other's actions," Seth assured me. "Were you involved in any of your parents' illegal dealings?"

I shook my head. "No, never."

"Do you plan on following in their footsteps now that they're gone?"

"Absolutely not." I grimaced. "It makes me a crap daughter to admit this out loud, but a part of me was relieved when they died because I didn't have to worry about them trying to pull me into one of their scams ever again."

"Good, that's all I needed to know." Seth pulled me off Jared's lap for a hug, and a deep growl rumbled up my mate's chest. Seth set me on my feet and took a step back, jerking his chin in Jared's direction. "That and the fact you're this guy's mate. I've already said this, but it bears repeating...you're a welcome addition to my pack."

Jared stood and wrapped his arms around me as I whispered, "Thank you."

"Now that we've cleared all that up, go knock her up," Seth instructed with a grin. "My son or daughter could use a playmate close to their age."

"Son or daughter?" I gasped, my eyes widening. "Is Jane pregnant?"

Seth pressed his finger to his lips as he glanced at the stairs that led up to the bedrooms. "Keep the news to yourselves for now. I know she was looking forward to telling you herself."

"Sure thing, boss." Jared tossed me over his shoulder and carried me to the truck.

"It's only been a week," I reminded him.

He swiped his thumb across my bottom lip. "A day, week, month, or year. It makes no difference since we're going to spend the rest of our lives with each other."

EPILOGUE

JARED

As an only child of only children, Rory had always wanted a big family. I was more than happy to give one to her, especially since I'd wanted a sibling when I was younger. After two pups in five years and another on the way, we were off to a great start...even though our house was hectic twenty-four seven.

Burying my face in my mate's hair, I wrapped my arms tighter around her lush body. Unfortunately, the days of lazy mornings in bed with Rory were long past, especially since our son liked getting up at sunrise. "Please tell me that the toilet flush I just heard was part of a dream. It took me until past midnight to get Layla down. I'm not ready to wake up yet."

Twisting her neck to offer me a sleepy smile, Rory murmured, "You would have gotten plenty of sleep if our darling daughter didn't have you wrapped around her little finger. Your mom and I have both told you it's okay to let her cry it out sometimes."

I was fearless in battle, but the sound of my daughter's cry had the power to break me. There was no use denying that I caved every time Layla blinked up at me with the same golden eyes I adored in her mom. Shaking my head with a sigh, I replied, "You know I can't do that to my daddy's girl, just like you can't hold out when Perry wants a new toy."

"We made some seriously cute kids." Rory pressed her lips together before admitting, "Too cute for our own good, judging by the new bike I ordered for Perry yesterday. Julian got one, so of course our son wanted the same kind."

Perry and Julian were growing up much the same way Seth and I had, glued to each other's side for as many hours in the day as we'd let them play together. When they got into mischief, my parents liked to remind me that it was payback for all the trouble we'd managed to get into when we were young.

"Remind me to talk to Seth about laying down the law when it comes to where they're allowed to ride those bikes," I muttered.

Rory patted my chest. "Jane already beat you to it. Seth said he'll have a talk with the boys, alpha to future alpha and beta."

"Good call." The boys were only five, but it was already clear they were destined to lead the pack when Seth and I were ready to step down—many, many years from now. Their wolves bristled with dominance, and they had already learned to depend on each other. Having the chance to teach them the same lessons our fathers had given us was one of my favorite parts of being a dad.

Rory dropped her hand down to her rounded belly. "I wonder what this one will be like."

"Since we already have little replicas of each of us, they'll probably be the perfect blend of us." I pressed my hand next to hers, smiling when the baby kicked hard against my palm. "Your golden eyes with my dark hair."

"Or your gorgeous blue eyes with my dark blond hair," she suggested with a smile.

"Whichever combination, we'll love them with our whole hearts."

Our son tested that love when he pounded on our bedroom door, loud enough that he was likely to wake his little sister. "Mommy, let me in. I want cuddles."

Rolling over with a groan, I climbed off the mattress and stalked to the door. Flinging it open, I shushed Perry. "Shh, if you wake up Layla this early, you'll be the one who changes her diaper."

"Eww." He wrinkled his nose. "Nuh-uh. No diaper. Make sis pee and poop in the potty."

"You didn't finish potty training until you were almost three, kiddo. She's not even two yet. Cut her some slack." I ruffled his hair, and then he darted past me to climb onto the mattress with his mom.

"Daddy's bein' mean, Mommy," he complained as he cuddled against her side, taking over my spot in bed. "I no wanna change Laylay's diaper."

"Don't worry, sweetie. Daddy was just joking around." She beamed a teasing smile at me. "You're too little, and I'm too big because of the baby. But your dad is just right, so he's the one who'll take care of your sister when she wakes up."

"Like the bears from my book," Perry squealed.

"Yup." Rory yawned. "And like Goldilocks, we found the perfect bed. So we're going to stay right here and get more sleep."

"I better be part of that plan," I grumbled as I slid under the covers and tickled our son's side. "Or else I'll have to huff and puff."

Perry giggled and shook his head. "That's not the right story, Daddy."

Although I'd read both books to him a couple of hundred times, I widened my eyes in surprise. "It isn't?"

"Nuh-uh."

"I guess Daddy is going to be on story-time duty tonight so you can teach him which book is which," Rory suggested, her eyes drifting shut.

Perry tilted his head back to smile at me. "Will you? Please?"

"Of course, kiddo." I flicked the end of his nose. "But only if you try to get a little more sleep since your mommy is so tired."

"Okay, Daddy," he agreed, squeezing his eyes shut.

My ploy worked, and I drifted off to sleep again...until my daddy's girl decided she'd had enough of her crib and wanted cuddles in our bed too.

Curious about the situation in Screaming Woods that Adan Deville was worried about? You can find out all about it—and see a little more of Adan—in Demon's Own!

Don't forget to join my newsletter to get free ebooks, special offers, and giveaways.

ABOUT THE AUTHOR

I absolutely adore reading—always have and always will. When I was growing up, my friends used to tease me when I would trail after them, trying to read and walk at the same time. If I have downtime, odds are you will find me reading or writing.

I am the mother of two wonderful sons who have inspired me to chase my dream of being an author. I want them to learn from me that you can live your dream as long as you are willing to work for it.

When I told my mom that my new year's resolution was to self-publish a book in 2013, she pretty much told me, "About time!"

Printed in Great Britain
by Amazon

21769270R00059